FAMILY VACATION MALFUNCTION

By

ANITA PASSON

International Standard Book Number 13: 978-1-60452-032-3
International Standard Book Number 10: 1-60452-032-9

Library of Congress Control Number: 2009904542

BluewaterPress LLC
2220 CR 210 W Ste 108 #132
Jacksonville, FL 32559
http://bluewaterpress.com

This book may be purchased online at -

http://bluewaterpress.com/vacation
or through
amazon.com

For Megan who makes me laugh,
For Daniel who makes me wonder,
For Jerry who makes me hope.

For the captain of our ship and our parents
who give us cakes, Fords, and a sense of humor.

For all families who hope for
the perfect family vacation.

Thank you, Susan, for creating
the perfect design for my book cover.
Your work is the icing on my cake!

And for Julie…
Yes, Julie, the book is finished…
and the turkey is in the oven.

Author's Note

It is my hope that this book will be incorporated in many classrooms as a "first week back to school" story, encouraging classroom discussion and ample writing and illustrating opportunities for students. *Family Vacation Malfunction*, affords ample opportunities to review or introduce prediction, figurative language, Venn diagrams, research, vocabulary instruction, and narrative writing.

It is an excellent tool for opening the communication lines among students and creating a positive classroom environment for your new school year. I have included some literature suggestions in the back of the book to use in conjunction with this story, and I look forward to reading Chapter 23 ½ from many students! Enjoy!

FAMILY VACATION MALFUNCTION

Chapter 1
Mickey Mouse Pancakes

My sister threw up Mickey Mouse pancakes on the way home from our family vacation in Florida. A rainbow of vomit erupted over Mount Megan's suntanned chin splattering my white Nike Shox and the DVDs camouflaging the floor mats of our 2001 Ford Taurus. It wasn't the kind of throwing up announced by the short, gaggy, warning cough that gives your victims time to sound the barf alarm. It was the explosive, take immediate cover, type. One minute Megan was watching a Barney video, and the next she was puking up a breakfast milkshake like magma spewing out of a volcano. My mom jerked the glove compartment open and grabbed the white, emergency restaurant napkins.

"We're out of napkins! Throw me your shirt… **NOW!**" screeched my mother as serious as an overtime goal, forcing the surrender of the lucky polo I'd been using as a pillow. My eyes bugged out of their sockets as she carefully positioned my brand new shirt under Megan's locked jaw like a heavy duty paper towel.

Two hours earlier I sat slouched in an overly air-conditioned Cracker Barrel in Chattanooga, Tennessee, staring as Megan shoveled Mickey Mouse pancakes masked in maple syrup, M & Ms, and whipped cream into bulging chipmunk cheeks. The scent of its sickening sweetness blanketed me with nausea.

Breakfast is the meal I eliminate during the summer months because I'm on the, sleep till noon schedule. But when you're on a family road trip, you quickly learn to eat and use the restrooms whenever your vehicle comes to a halt. So, I forced this foreign meal down, knowing that a mid- afternoon Taco Bell request would be as ignored as the annoying student waving his hand in the air while my teacher is trying to explain an assignment.

While my step-dad parted with two more Andrew Jacksons, I body slammed the exit door, plowing into the June heat like it was a defenseman twice my size. I trudged in slow motion across the steaming parking lot, struggling to break free from Mother Nature's heated grip. Regurgitated breakfast was the last thing on my mind as our vehicle merged onto the northbound highway headed for our mitten state.

My step-dad jerked my thoughts back to the present as he swiftly swerved the car over to the right hand lane after spotting a billboard advertising several restaurants at the next exit. I dug my finger tips deep into my mother's head rest as we plunged under the green light at the bottom of the ramp, and into the entrance of a Wendy's restaurant where our car halted seconds before kissing the yellow parking block.

Four doors frantically flung open as I scrambled out, giving my mom space to reach in, unlatch the car seat, and rescue Megan from the puking section. While she raced to the women's restroom, I sprinted towards the condiments and straws area, greedily grabbing napkins from the dispenser before speeding back to the car where my step- dad was scooping up the most important meal of the day with the beach towels that had been shoved in the back corner of the trunk.

There are certain family vacation memories that a thirteen year old boy treasures in the hopes of sharing with his own children some day...this would not be one of them.

Chapter 2
My Family Gives Me Indigestion

Most families go on vacation to, *get away from it all.* My family will never be able to do this because the, *it all, is* my family. We would have to bring in substitute family members to avoid our annual misery marathon more commonly known as, *the family vacation.* My mom claims that my brother, sister, and I clash because of age differences she refers to as, *the terrible threes* (my sister skipped the terrible twos), *the annoying eights, and the trying teens.*

This might help explain why I always end up with a serious case of indigestion whenever we go out to eat. While waiting for our order, it's routine for Daniel and Megan to kick the snot out of one another under the table until it jerks toppling my glass of Mountain Dew, usually onto a tiled floor where it shatters into a bazillion pieces. Their annoying antics aggravate my stomach so much that by the time my hot roast beef sandwich with double taters arrives, my stomach is too knotted to enjoy it.

If my family couldn't get through sixty minutes of dinner without a meltdown, how could we possibly endure an entire week of one another's company? Each summer I pondered this dilemma as our vacation drew nearer, but this summer a theory so ingenious hit me like a puck to the helmet while my grandpa was describing his claustrophobic episode in one of those x-ray machines. He said people with claustrophobia can get really freaked out when they feel trapped in a tight place like an elevator or the tunnel he was describing.

That was it! My *family* freaked out when *we* were trapped *with one another*! A small part of my brain lit up, pinging and ringing like a pinball machine. During the regular school year there were always five *different schedules* going on, each of us coming and going at *different times* (except for Sunday church and an occasional brunch afterwards), but summer vacation meant *one* family schedule and spending large blocks of time, *together.* I named my new theory, *family phobia: anxiety caused by the close proximity of annoying family members.*

As my grandpa continued describing his tunnel experience, it occurred to me that this problem didn't exist until my younger brother was born. In fact, the *only* vacation that I ever enjoyed was *before* he was born. Well, it wasn't exactly a vacation. I was three years old and my mom felt guilty about leaving me with my grandparents while she and my new step-dad went honeymooning, so the newlyweds planned a little get away to Kings Island in Cincinnati, Ohio. I remember my favorite ride, the miniature roller coaster, and meeting my favorite cartoon character, Scooby Doo. I even had my photo put on the cover of a sports magazine which I still have in a plastic frame on the desk in my bedroom.

But three years later, the seeds of family phobia began to take root… like poison ivy. We went on our first family outing with Daniel to the amusement park, Cedar Point, in Sandusky, Ohio. He was almost two years old with blonde hair and skin as white as whole milk.

As soon as we entered the park my mom pulled him aside and greased him from head to toe with maximum sun protection, one- hundred, so he wouldn't fry like bacon in a skillet. An hour later, Daniel rubbed his eyes with chubby little hands lathered in two coatings of UV protection, and started shrieking like someone was trying to steal his cheeseburger Happy Meal. While my parents frantically searched for the emergency area, I dragged a few steps behind, hoping bystanders wouldn't realize I was with, *The Sun Tan Lotion Kid*. Of course, once we arrived, Daniel kicked and pushed away anyone who tried to get within three feet of his eyes to help him.

A disheartening, deflated feeling washed over me as I stood staring and waiting for his tears to rinse away the lotion that was supposed to have prevented him from boiling like a lobster. For the first time in my life, I questioned the reality of *fun* family getaways. Were they just imaginary pictures that parents painted to get you into the car, or did they truly exist? Not only had Daniel ruined my day, but he'd jabbed a pin through another one of my childhood fantasies.

Since then, Daniel's knack for getting on my parents' nerves had been as annoying as a cheap shot in hockey. He was five and I was ten years old when our sister, Megan, was born, downgrading Daniel's status from baby of the family to the dreaded, middle child. And you know what they say about the middle child always getting the short end of the stick, a hand-me-down stick, at that.

I decided that this summer's family vacation would be the perfect opportunity to discover the truth behind our family vacation malfunctions. An eighteen hour road trip from Monroe, Michigan to Lady Lake, Florida, and seven days in the sunshine state would give me the time I needed to diagnose my family's vacation malady. Did my family suffer from family phobia, or was there *one member* solely responsible for sabotaging our vacations? This would be the summer I would discover the truth.

Although I secretly wished that our vacation could imitate the Disney World commercial where the perfect family saunters down Main Street holding hands and giggling, I realized that this would call for a radical behavior transfusion.

The question was: Did Disney World possess enough enchantment for such a severe transformation?

Chapter 3
Droopy Bottom Woes

Our road trip began on a Friday afternoon in June, two weeks into every kid's favorite time of the year, SUMMER VACATION! Shortly after placing my carefully selected video games and movies into my assigned space, I spotted a potentially dangerous situation. I stood gaping at our car's sagging bottom, the result of a trunk so crammed with suitcases, duffle bags, snacks, and golf clubs that it looked like it could pop a wheelie any minute.

I didn't dare share this observation with my crazed mother who'd sprung out of bed that morning like a hockey player sprinting from the penalty box back to his bench. While visions of golf courses danced in my head, she had made some last minute purchases at our local twenty-four hour Meijer, and repacked each of our clean, but embarrassingly stained and holey pairs of underwear and socks, with dazzling, white replacements just in case they turned up on my grandparents' living room carpet.

If there was a law limiting snack and beverage quantities on board moving vehicles, we would have been in serious violation. Wherever there was an extra inch of foot space my mom had expertly crammed packages of Cheezits, granola bars, beef jerky, peanuts, and gummy snacks, bottles of water, and my step-dad's caffeinated co-pilot, Coca Cola. I predicted that I would have no feeling in both legs and feet by the time we crossed the Michigan/ Ohio state line.

A silent count down began as I stifled the guilt in my gut from not sharing the droopy tushy information. As my mom carefully backed our vehicle down the driveway and into the street of our quiet, meticulously manicured neighborhood, my thoughts screamed,

"Ten, nine, eight... Pull back, pull back! Seven, six, five... Abort mission! Abort mission! Four... malfunction in the back bumper! Three... I can't sit in this car for eighteen hours! Two... I'm already feeling family phobic! One... Let me out!"

The garage door slowly descended leaving our disappointed van draped in darkness. Our 1998 Windstar had never given us any reason to doubt her abilities to safely transport our family to any given destination. Okay, so she had put on a few miles over the past five years, but was this good enough reason for abandoning her for a newer vehicle, and depriving her of a trip to Disney World? I thought this was an inconsiderate, not to mention, idiotic decision; an unexpected call from two college graduates who must have been absent the day the common sense lesson was taught.

Our Taurus grabbed the road like a teenager who's been handed the keys to the family car for the first time.

But as her speedometer gage ascended, so did anxiety levels in my tight chest as unnerving thoughts unleashed a flurry of panic:

"What if my body suddenly shifted into high gear in the next twenty-four hours triggering my long awaited growth spurt, and here I was stuffed in a box with no room for expansion?"

I was the smallest boy in a class that had been together since preschool. A lot of my classmates had already transformed into teenagers with pimpled faces and gangly limbs that looked like they'd been stretched on some medieval torturing device. I needed some major alterations before next fall, or my clear complexion and eighty pounds of puniness would start drawing as much attention as a fire alarm blasting in a school hallway. I made up my mind to fight for every inch of space at the slightest signs of growth. If my siblings put up resistance, I would retaliate with as many silent body slams and finger nail gougings necessary to encourage my metamorphosis.

I was relieved that I still had feeling in both legs and feet, with no signs of tingling, as we entered the buckeye state. Our car detoured west to Maumee, Ohio to retrieve the captain of our ship, my step-dad, who had gone into work for a half day.

My step-dad looked as excited as a kid bursting through the doors on the last day of school. He was eager to see his parents and had, *"Let's get this show on the road"* painted across his forehead. However, the words became blurred with hues of pink and red as his dark eyes spotted the droopy bottom situation. Steam blew out of his ears like a train from a Saturday morning cartoon as he stared wide-eyed, first at the lopsided vehicle, and then at me.

You know that feeling you get when the teacher is writing on the chalkboard and your best friend makes that fart noise with his hands, and then she spins around and makes eye contact with you, and threatens to take away second recess if somebody doesn't rat on the hand farter? It was just like that.

I should have ratted on the golf clubs.

For the past several weeks my parents had debated (quite loudly), whether or not to take the golf clubs. Why couldn't my step-dad and I just *borrow* some from one of my grandparents' neighbors? Finding someone to lend us golf clubs in a retirement village in Florida would be as easy as scoring a goal when the goalie is pulled. But when the bitter battle broke it was as clear as freshly zambonied ice that the clubs would not be left behind, a decision deserving of, at the very least, a game misconduct. Unfortunately, our vehicle's back bumper was serving the penalty for one parent's preoccupation with playing with his *own* clubs.

I felt a momentary pang of remorse for my selfishness (I like to refer to it as self concern). I had observed the over- burdened bottom, severely aware that the golf clubs had put us over the limit, and had kept this information classified knowing how important they were to my step-dad's (and yes, my own), personal happiness. My guilt quickly subsided however, as my feet turned into two concrete blocks.

Besides, there was no reason for *me* to feel guilty when it was clearly my *parents'* poor judgment that was at the root of our pathetic predicament. If *they* had chosen to drive the more experienced vehicle, and purchased the Big Mac container for the roof, we all would be enjoying the comfort and security of our trusty old van. My investigation took a twisted turn as *my parents* became my primary suspects.

Chapter 4
Surf's Up!

We drove as far as Lexington, Kentucky where we camped out at a Holiday Inn. The next morning, dangerous downpours and hurricane- like winds pelted our windshield as Mother Nature wore the blade of my step-dad's patience right down to the boot. Our car became a surfboard plunging under gallons of water, scrambling for air as her windshield wipers' most valiant efforts were defeated. As soon as she'd finish riding out one wave, another would crash, jilting us off the highway. I turned the volume on my CD player up to high hoping to drown out the treacherous weather, my step dad's unrepeatable adjectives, and the annoying,

"Mom, he's touching me again!" marathon going on beside me. The portable DVD player offered little relief for my brother and me since our parents had given Megan exclusive rights to movie choices.

I stared blankly at the screen while the music from my headphones drowned the *Scooby Dooby Doo* theme music blasting from the DVD player. Even though I kept hoping that Megan would nod off just long enough to watch one of our, *inappropriate for three- year -olds,* movies, I felt a little sorry for my Little Monkey (my nickname for her). Our parents had strategically placed her as a human force field (more like a human sacrifice), between Daniel and me, thinking this would prevent us from pounding and kicking the tar out of one another. When Megan finally drifted off for one or two hours at a time, we popped in an Adam Sandler movie with the volume so low we resorted to lip reading, although we knew all of the lines by heart.

Mother Nature's fury tacked on three *additional* hours of driving time, which included several pit stops at rest areas to let our car catch her breath. Her heavy bottom was making it difficult to keep the tires afloat, and that wasn't the only problem. Shortly after crossing the Georgia state line, my step-dad announced that he'd lost feeling in both arms. This made me a little nervous. He was the captain of our vessel, and even though my mother sat in the co-captain's chair, my Yorkshire, Reese's natural instincts would have been better able to navigate our family safely to my grandparents' home.

Chapter 5
And the Clock Struck Twelve...

Our weary Taurus released an explosive sigh of relief like the uncapping of four, shaken two-liter Coke bottles as we safely landed on my grandparents' driveway. She had overcome twenty-one death defying hours of Mother Nature's energy sucking wrath, and succeeded in safely delivering her family to their Floridian destination. She deserved, without a doubt, the Most Valuable Player Award.

It was 11:45 *P.M.* when we finally collapsed all over my grandparents' living room with our assortment of empty fast food bags and various pieces of mismatched luggage. My mamaw had probably spent the last few days dusting, vacuuming, and Windexing, and now you couldn't even tell with all of our stuff plopped everywhere throughout a room which normally looked like a photograph straight out of one of those country home magazines.

Moments after our arrival, the embarrassing character flaws, bad habits, and savage behavior that my mother had repeatedly threatened us not to reveal, spurted out of Megan and Daniel like a garden hose gone out of control.

Bad habits are like stubborn carpet stains that you try to remove with cheap cleaner from a spray bottle. The carpet appears clean on the surface, but the stains sink deep into the padding, resulting in irreparable damage. My mom had tried to spray away our bad habits before our arrival, but they quickly became as apparent as red wine on white carpet.

I knew from the moment she began babbling about being on our best behavior that it would be a mission impossible. Eliminating an occasional, *stupid* or *albino* comment seemed a reasonable request, but asking us to go *cold turkey* from my siblings most enjoyable pastime, insulting one another until we face off in head to head combat, was going to present an interesting challenge. What would fill my time in between golfing, swimming, and Disney World theme parks? And worse, without agitating remarks about Daniel's nerdy, wire-rimmed glasses and spare tire protruding over his swimsuit, he might begin to think I'd accepted him as my equal, worthy of heated topics involving World Series and NHL champions. No, this was not a request I was capable of granting, not even to a mother who dangled my future car keys from her fingertips.

My siblings' humiliating display of dysfunction was hilarious. Each scrambled to my mamaw's piano competing for the bench while demonstrating a variety of push, pull, shove, scratch, and pinch techniques. Megan succeeded in occupying the bench first, and began pounding unrecognizable chords while Daniel screamed, "You're so stupid! Move over! You don't even know how to play!" (Daniel's resume included six months of piano lessons.)

Watching my mortified parents squirm in embarrassment while attempting to defuse each episode with some psychological reasoning (instead of their usual screaming at the top of their lungs and lame threats involving television, video games, or both), was more entertaining than any movie. For a moment I thought that the two of *them* might cave in to the very language we'd been threatened to avoid at all costs.

They were both mentally fried; especially my step-dad who'd successfully driven the entire road trip while never once losing his ability to whip his almighty arm around and blindly slam any obnoxious behavior coming from the rear of the car, a talent all fathers, and in my case, some mothers possess.

My mamaw extinguished both fires as each softened from road trip fatigue. I'm sure that my mamaw and papaw figured that we were all, *a little out of sorts,* from our horrendous drive.

Maybe this trip wouldn't live up to my fantasy family vacation, and I might not even discover the culprit responsible for our lack of vacation fun, *but I knew one thing.* When my grandparents realized that our family's, *out of sorts* behavior, was the *only* behavior we practiced, this *could* prove to be the most *entertaining* family vacation ever!

Chapter 6
Magic Kingdom? We'll Need Four Servings

It was one of those rainy Sundays where you lie around the living room watching TV and munching all day. It was just what I needed: some serious recuperation time. No one in my family rolled out of bed until almost eleven o'clock. Of course, my grandparents had probably been up since the crack of dawn, anxious for the rest of us to join the land of the living. Sleeping this late on a Sunday felt awkward because my family usually attended the 10:30 mass at our church. My mom would probably make us go to church twice when we got back home to make up for our absence.

We spent the day talking and watching my papaw channel surf. We watched, *The Little Mermaid* and *Cinderella* from Megan's movie collection, but when I asked if we could watch one of *my* movies my mom gave me the,

"Drop it, Mamaw and Papaw will flip out if they see the kind of movies you watch!" death glare.

My mamaw made a delicious roast beef dinner with real (not the boxed kind), mashed potatoes and gravy and a corn casserole, and after that we laid around some more just waiting for our food to digest so that we could make some ice cream sundaes. When I finally climbed into bed, I was so rested and so stuffed that I couldn't get to sleep, so I waited until my papaw turned off all the lights, and then I sneaked out to watch one of my, inappropriate for grandparents movies, until two a.m.

* * *

Six hours later, I forced my rubbery legs back into our recovering vehicle, and resumed my assigned seat where my personal cheek indentations remained from the previous two days of intense travel. Despite another forty-five minutes of driving, I looked forward to a pit stop at one of my favorite breakfast restaurants, Perkins, before boarding the ferry bound for one of the most famous theme parks in the world.

Anxiety levels were high as we dragged our breakfast-filled stomachs and scrambled towards the crowded trolley lines which would transport us to the ferry, and ultimately, The Magic Kingdom. My mom chose one line, and my step-dad chose another which, *was suspiciously shorter,* than the rest. Eventually, my mom backed down (but not before a few moments of parental pouting), and joined his line, which we discovered, *wasn't actually a line* at all. It was just a bunch of clueless people like us trying to figure this whole process out. My mom dropped a couple of sarcastic bomb shells just to let him know that she was always right, and we pushed our way over to the end of an *official* trolley line. This embarrassing episode cost us about ten minutes of theme park time, which I knew my mom would never let my step-dad forget.

When our trolley finally arrived, my step-dad boarded first, clutching Megan tightly to his chest like she was a bank bag filled with a million dollars. My mom followed next, lugging the stroller, video recorder, camera, backpack, and kitchen sink, followed by klutzy Daniel, tripping over his own feet. I hopped in last, and accidentally on purpose, successfully executed the, *body shove-elbow to the side maneuver,* while skillfully escaping Daniel's lame retaliation jab.

With the heat index fast approaching one hundred degrees, my mother lathered Daniel with sun protection number fifty (she only lathered from his elbows up this time). As beads of perspiration glistened off my bronzed body, I couldn't tell if his sensitive skin was turning pink from the sun, or from the embarrassment of being lathered by his mommy in front of perfect strangers.

My mother completed the lathering process just in time for us to scamper off the trolley with hundreds of other frenzied folks darting towards the ferry. She hauled all of the paraphernalia down the steps, and joined the crowd's frantic pace while Daniel and I trailed a few steps behind. I kept my eyes so focused that they burned as I struggled to keep my parents in sight. I had no idea how nervy the whole process of getting to the Magic Kingdom was. Being separated from our parents this early in the day would have triggered a parental meltdown of mammoth proportions.

I spotted the famous Disney icon towering through an awesome blue sky as our ferry approached the enchanted kingdom. We followed the packs of dripping Disney fans scurrying off the ferry like Cinderella's mice in pursuit of aged cheese, and pushed our way through the park's entrance and down Main Street, determined to reach

Cinderella's castle as if there was some prize to be won at the finish line.

My parents skillfully ambled our family in and out of sun drenched tourists towards a spectacular display of Disney characters singing and dancing to some funky hip hop music. Fans crammed the streets straining to view the spectacle of princesses and villains. It was like being at a rock concert, except for the part where the average spectator was six years old clutching a Disney hand held fan that misted water at sweaty little faces.

Steam rose from my new shoes as I peered down to check on them. My tolerance for heat and crowds is lower than a hockey player's self esteem after being chewed up by the coach for a costly penalty. I'd rather skate at full force wearing only my boxers down a Michigan rink, than push my way through the hot, crowded streets of a Florida theme park in mid June.

My thoughts were rudely interrupted by a stocky, middle-aged, shiny bald as a bowling ball man complaining about not being able to see over *certain* parents whose children were perched on their shoulders. I glanced over at Megan balancing on my step-dad's shoulders, her tanned, little legs bouncing against his chest to the rhythm of the music. As perspiration rained down her forehead, over her long dark lashes, and into the corners of her brown eyes as large as one of Mrs. Pott's saucers, I thought to myself,

"Not today, Baldy!"

I edged towards the whining, pathetic man and glared at him with Herculean laser burning power until he could feel my fury. He turned, glanced in my direction, and shifted into another area of the crowd. I hoped he felt ashamed of himself, carrying on like an overly-tired toddler when there were so many kids like my Little Monkey mesmerized by the magical performance. I made a mental note to take Megan off my list of suspects. No one that young and innocent could possibly be the cause of our family's vacation dilemma. Could they?

Chapter 7
Ungrateful Teenager

White heat shimmered and sweat trickled into my lashes like a slow dripping faucet, making me see black sun spots. I felt like the character, Iago, from the movie, *Aladdin,* screeching, "I'm molting! I'm molting!"

I couldn't afford to shed any more pounds. I needed to find some shade, and fast! As I dragged my fatigued feet to the next attraction: *Story Time with Belle,* I couldn't help wondering if I should have stayed home with my mamaw and papaw, hanging by the pool with all the retired sun goddesses sipping peach flavored iced-teas.

My parents halted in their heated tracks. A dragon-like fireball of anger scorched the tips of my spiked, sun-bleached hair. I turned abruptly and glanced behind hoping their fury was directed towards someone else. Maybe, a whacked out mother had run over my step-dad's heel with a baby stroller.

I quickly scanned Daniel's dancing dark eyes for help and made a horrific discovery. His raised brows and puckered cheeks could barely contain his satisfaction. He salivated smugness like a dog drooling in front of a pound of raw hamburger. This could only mean one thing. My, *Only Child Who Hadn't Ticked His Parents Off On Our Vacation,* title had been stripped. An unidentifiable force had cheap shotted me, leaving me dazed and stunned. But what unspeakable crime had I committed to dip so low in the rankings? I quickly retraced my thoughts… my thoughts…. **MY THOUGHTS**! They hadn't been thoughts at all! I had actually spoken those ungrateful, I *wish I wasn't here even though you spent tons of money on this vacation,* thoughts.

But how could this have happened? I had been on such a roll, especially after the, *Daniel and Megan Late Show* from the night before. I was a young Steve Yzerman from the Detroit Red Wings at the top of his game. But within seconds, I had become as popular as the least desired draft pick. It must have been the heat! It had taken control of me, and put me in some sort of trance just long enough to utter those ungrateful and unappreciative thoughts. Oh, how I hated the heat!

The words hung in the hot heavy humidity. I tried waving them away like tiny annoying gnats, but they wouldn't evaporate; the overcrowded water molecules wouldn't make room for them. I dragged my limp body along, listening, but not listening, as my parents' badgering dropped in and out like a poor phone connection,

"…spoiled, rotten…don't know why we…should have…" blah, blah, blah. I glared at Daniel who was still basking in his new found status. But this time I kept my thoughts guarded,

"Enjoy yourself for now, Daniel, because we're headed for Fantasyland where we'll be trapped for the rest of the day, immersed in elephants, elves, and evil villains. We'll see how long *your* reign of popularity prevails."

I was a chained and shackled captive marching into the Fantasyland of Disney's Magic Kingdom, a teenage prisoner who had committed such an unthinkable crime that it would take more enchantment than even Walt possessed to save me.

Chapter 8
Dumbo and Snow White and Alice... Oh No!

Clutching the Belle doll she whined and cried over until my parents broke like china on concrete and purchased, Miss Megan began dictating the family's itinerary as she directed us towards a land of characters and creatures definitely missing from *my* starting lineup.

"Here, take this, and grab a couple lemonades, and sit with your brother over there for a few minutes." My mother shoved a five dollar bill into my sweaty hand and pointed us towards an area where there were small tables shaded by huge, yellow umbrellas. Daniel and I plunked down and gulped our sour lemonades while the day flashed before my eyes like a carousel on fast foward.

I stared as my step-dad entered the Dumbo ride line, and wondered how a man with the patience of Shear Khan could withstand waiting in one-hundred-five degrees, feel like you're gulping carbon dioxide, heat, hugging my sister to his dripping polo shirt while my mother proudly stood by videotaping Megan like it was her wedding day!

Afterwards, we followed Megan over to the Snow White's Scary Adventures attraction where we packed into the dwarves' mine ride and traveled through scenes from the Snow White movie. Hopelessness swallowed me as I wondered if I'd ever escape from Fantasyland.

Moments after exiting the mine car, as if she was reading my mind, my mother quickly paraded our family out of Fantasyland and over to Tomorrowland and Buzz Lightyear's Space Ranger Spin! My relief was short lived however, when she immediately directed us *back* to Fantasyland after pulling some little tickets out of a machine. I became more discouraged and angrier than ever, now that I had seen the awesome rides I was missing out on, all because of the three- year -old queen bee.

My mother informed us that we had time for two more rides before lunch, so she invited Daniel and me to join them on the Mad Tea Party. My unexpected enthusiasm dumbfounded Daniel who shot me a puzzled look. I responded with a quick, *trust me,* wink, anticipating the ride would make Megan so dizzy she would surrender control of the morning's agenda. A stroke of genius, or so I thought.

Unfortunately, *I* became the victim of the twirling teacups as my stomach and I played tug-o-war with my Perkins blueberry pancakes. As I tightly closed my eyes, trying to shut out the blurring colors, I heard the distinctive giggling of a certain traitorous toddler,

"Make it go faster, Daddy!"

No way! My plan had backfired, just like my pancakes would if this ride didn't end soon. As I stumbled out of the cup and staggered over to the exit door (and the nearest trash can), I forced my rolling eyes to focus on Megan's teacup. Lucky for her, my dad had whisked her into his protective arms, saving her from the uncomfortable faltering. My fists clenched while my top and bottom braces ground uncontrollably:

Three- year- old *innocent* damsel? I may have had ten years on her, but she had total control of the game! And my parents' preoccupation with the youngest sibling's happiness was blowing my whole family phobic theory right out of the water. Daniel and I had become the bench warmers on a team where three players were having the game of their lives!

Well, bring it on. Bench warming wasn't an activity I was familiar with, and I didn't plan to get too comfortable. Sooner or later our young All Star would run out of gas, and when that happened I would be more than ready to jump in for the substitution.

Chapter 9
Fast Pass Power

My parents purchased a lemonade for Megan after the Teacup fiasco, and we wasted some more time under one of those over-sized umbrellas while her battery recharged. And, of course, she had to go to the bathroom after that!

When Megan and my mom returned from the ladies restroom, she announced that we had ten minutes to book it over to Tomorrowland, or we'd lose the chance to use our fasts passes and would have to reschedule for later in the day. Fast passes? What was she talking about?

I soon learned that fast passes are ride tickets you pull out of a machine at the more popular attractions. They list a time to return to the fast pass lane instead of the longer, regular line. When we had hiked over to the Buzz Lightyear attraction earlier, I remembered seeing a digital sign that said there was a forty-five minute wait, but the ticket my mom was handing me now said that our ride was for 1:15 where there would be, *a no minute wait*!

Whoever came up with this idea should be given a trillion dollar raise!

Trapped in an endless maze of lanes like mice in a laboratory experiment is a challenge for any family, but unbearably, agonizing for mine. These passes would totally eliminate some major family phobic episodes. There would be no stepping on Daniel's heels to prod him forward every few minutes, no Daniel finger flicking Megan's sunburned ears, and no retaliation shoves creating a domino effect where I'm knocked against annoyed strangers' sweaty bodies.

My mom's outstanding online research skills scored her enough points to scratch her completely off my list of suspects. It was obvious that she had anticipated our family's Achilles heel for theme parks, and had discovered the antidote before we experienced an outbreak of attraction line dysfunction.

Now I was getting somewhere. One down, three to go.

Chapter 10
Buzz Lightyear to MY Rescue!

As my mom pulled those life saving tickets out of her purse, we brushed past all the weary, irritated families sweating it out in the regular lines. I felt a little sorry for the kids whose faces were as green as dollar bills wishing *their* moms had gotten fast passes.

The corners of my mouth angled into an unfamiliar position as I carefully placed my hands on the shiny black wheel of my *personal* spaceship. Finally, I was in the game! No more bench warming for me. I jerked and twirled my star cruiser, shooting the laser canons like Al Capone with his trusty machine gun. I laughed out loud watching Megan aim at familiar enemies while my step-dad jerked their ship from side to side. This ride seemed to last longer than most; maybe because I was so hysterically happy! But then something happened making it deserving of an A+ grade, a grade I'd only seen in the Physical Education section of my report card.

There was a mix up getting us off the ride, so the attendants just told us to stay on for another go around!

Our family double dipping on an awesome ride like this? Now *I* was a recharged battery! The heat and the three-year -old cruise director had been sucking the life out of me all morning, and this ride had been the aspirin for my pounding, *what was I thinking coming to The Magic Kingdom,* headache.

Walt Disney designed Tomorrowland to show what he thought the future might be like someday. Could this incredible experience be any indication of my family's future as well?

Chapter 11
Enchanted Burgers

I've always wondered what life was like behind the walls of Cinderella's castle; a curiosity, *probably not shared* by too many hockey players, so when my mom announced weeks before our vacation that she'd made 2:00 lunch reservations for the enchanted abode, I was relieved that I had a legitimate excuse for stepping foot inside the fairy tale home.

Immediately after the Buzz Lightyear euphoria, my mother directed our dragging, dehydrated bodies back to Fantasy Land and Cinderella's home. The castle's frigid air conditioning rescued us from the tormenting heat and humidity we had suffered all morning. I sucked the cold air in like a strawberry slurpy and began to feel more like myself again, (although according to my parents was *not necessarily a good thing*).

My mother checked in with the hostess, while my dad and Daniel and I dropped onto a bench to wait for our name to be called. Megan plopped down on Cindy's regal throne, knowing my mother wouldn't miss this, once in a lifetime Kodak moment. While my mom was finishing up Megan's photo shoot our name was announced, and we scurried over to the elevator and began our ascent to the top floor.

The elevator door slid open to reveal the ultimate Disney dining experience: dozens of young men and women bustling from table to table, balancing large round trays of enchanted food on their shoulders and flashing smiles like the Cheshire cat from *Alice in Wonderland.* The young waitresses sparkled in their golden gowns while the waiters strutted starched white shirts and pants that stopped at their knees. I stared past the flurry of movement, miles up towards the vaulted ceiling, and then down again where my eyes remained transfixed on the rainbow of colors streaking through the churchlike stained glass windows. I almost toppled backwards trying to drink in every detail as I pulled out the heavy, high backed, wooden chair.

"What would you like to drink, my lord?"

Was she referring to *me* as, *my lord*? I felt like throwing both arms in the air and yelling, "YES!"

Finally, somebody cared about what *I* wanted!

Our drinks were served in golden, glass goblets, not those plastic throw away cups that you get at most burger places. While I inhaled my cola, I spied several mammoth cheeseburgers being served to a family who looked as exhausted as ours, and I sensed that there was a burger with my name, laying in waiting in the fairy tale kitchen. And so, there was no doubt about what *this* lord desired to fill his noble stomach when the inquiry came,

"And what selection has my lord decided upon?"

Inhaling my bodacious burger prepared especially for me, with fries shaped like mini waffles, and gazing down at the commoners pounding the steaming sidewalks below... life didn't get much better than this. The enchanted castle possessed treasures beyond my expectations. When Sleeping Beauty and Belle whisked by flashing their perfect pearly whites and gloves, it was as if all symptoms of family phobia disappeared with a flick of their wrists.

This was the *second* time in one day that my family had enjoyed time *together* even though we sat close enough to sneak in a cheap jab, or a pinch of sarcasm. Had this palace cast a spell on my family and transformed us into that *commercial family*? Wasn't this the place where all your dreams come true?

Chapter 12
I Spoke Too Soon

Tempers flared shortly after scarfing down the last waffle fry when my mother realized she hadn't planned enough time between lunch and the afternoon parade to choose the ideal location to view the Disney spectacle. I was yanked back into reality so abruptly, I barely had enough time to take a Kodak mental picture to add to my meager file of pleasurable vacation memories. It was unsettling how quickly my mother shifted gears. The urgency in her voice shattered my surreal lunch like a hammer slamming against the evil queen's mirror in Snow White.

After several embarrassing moments of indecisiveness, my parents plunked us on a prime piece of land surrounded by large, red, bee attracting flowers My step-dad jokingly commented about all of the good places already being snatched up, and my mother retaliated with her deafening death stare.

Megan sat motionless in a trance- like state, staring wide eyed at characters she'd seen only in cartoons, singing and dancing in floats like those in Christmas parades on TV. I just kept wondering about the real folks inside the costumes. If I was hot enough to peel off my skin, I couldn't imagine how uncomfortable they were. Maybe they had portable air conditioning units in their suits.

Seconds after the parade, my mother whisked us off to the, *Jungle Cruise* and *It's A Small World,* where the rhythmic motions and music helped rock our little princess to sleep. And so, the day took an unexpected turn when the youngest sibling **SURRENDERED TO EXHAUSTION,** conking out in her umbrella stroller. I glanced at a nearby clock …5:45! Whew! She was finally out of the game!

My step-dad, the product of the equation heat times crowds equals mega stress, offered to sit with Megan in a shaded area, and that's when my mom looked at Daniel and me and asked,

"Do you guys want to head over to the Haunted Mansion?"

It was like skating into a wall at full speed. I had given up all hope of this attraction, and now my mom was handing it to me on a silver platter I wanted to scream,

"**YES, YES, YES**!" but no words would come. I shook my head so hard I felt like a bobble head figure. She took that for a yes, and we made a mad dash towards the mansion…and I made a mental note to bring a friend my own age the next time we came to this park. Elephants and teacups didn't cut it when you're three years away from driving your own carriage.

Chapter 13
Haunted Happenings

Unfortunately, the Haunted Mansion hadn't been included on the *princess's* itinerary, so we didn't have those awesome fast passes to save us the forty-five minute wait. I didn't mind though. This amazing attraction would bring one teenager more satisfaction than any tourist in the history of the Magic Kingdom because I was going to see Daniel spooked out of his mind!

Daniel's dilated pupils camouflaged his brown eyes. His raised brows indicated that he was in the fight or flight mode (more flight with Daniel), and his face was a lighter shade of albino. Watching him squirm as he cautiously advanced every few minutes towards the ominous mansion was as satisfying as teasing a slow defenseman trying to out -skate me to the net.

Tormenting cries poured over the walls as we warily crept towards the manor. Once inside, we joined an anxious mob where we were prodded like cattle into a circular room plastered with animated paintings of high society characters. There was no turning back now as the crowded chamber became a breathing room only facility. For a few moments I could relate to my Michigan grandpa's claustrophobic episode.

The startling movement of the floor lowering caused Daniel to falter as two doors burst open revealing blinding blackness. Cautiously, we edged into the darkness to wait for a car that would transport us through this phantom house. There was just one problem. In order to board one of these cars, the rider needed to cross a *moving turntable* and quickly jump into a car, *that was also moving.* This could be kind of tricky, even for a person as athletically gifted as me, but disastrous for an eight year old whose brain developed way before his gross motor skills. It would have been easier for Daniel to recite all of his multiplication facts than for him to attempt this next feat. My mother began desperately debriefing Daniel, explaining the, *cross a moving floor and jump into a moving car process.* He was shaking his head and showing sure signs of panic.

An unfamiliar sensation suddenly spread through my chest. Maybe my hamburger and waffle fries were exchanging blows, causing some delayed indigestion. No, this wasn't a physical reaction, it was... well... emotional, like in that Christmas movie when that guy's heart gets bigger. I felt...*concern* for my younger brother. I had had my fun up until this moment, but when it came down to this ultimate display of humiliation, I couldn't let him take the fall.

There was no time for a plan. I had to think fast. This wasn't my strong point. The car was impatient for us to board. I quickly pulled an unsuspecting Daniel away from my mother, and skillfully guided him as carefully as a puck on its way to the net. I took the steps for him as we glided in perfect sync. It happened so quickly that no one realized the heroic deed that had just taken place, no one, except Daniel.

As the bar came down to secure us, I heard a grateful sigh escape from my brother. The wailing walls couldn't drown out the relief that I felt for and from Daniel. While we were transported from one foreboding, phantom filled room to the next, I glanced over to find that his frightened facial features had relaxed, and when our car came to an abrupt halt, the wall of mirrors revealed Daniel and his friendly apparition with smiles on both of their faces.

While joining the other riders funneling towards the red exit sign, it occurred to me that Daniel and I had been the underdogs of the day. The players, *most likely not to succeed,* experiencing the magic of, *The Magic Kingdom.* Despite the fact that Daniel wore the genius pants of the team, as the older brother, I should have anticipated how hard it would be to please all three of us when there were such big age gaps inbetween us. I should have connived a plan convincing our parents of the benefits of Daniel and I separating from them for some agreed upon portion of the day. I could have even thrown in a little of,

"And you'll be able to enjoy some *quality time* with Megan without having to listen to Daniel and I complain," and they *may* have gone for it.

But, as often happens with teenagers, we live for the moment, never planning ahead for our next step... which often times is over the edge of a cliff.

Chapter 14
How Much Did You Say?

When we returned, Megan had just awakened from a sweaty, restless sleep in her stroller, and she was not a happy camper. Her hair was glued to her moist, tanned forehead, and her favorite little orange and pink sundress was stuck to her legs like a bandage that needs to be ripped off quickly. Luckily, we were just in time to whisk her off to, *The Liberty Tree Tavern,* for our seven o'clock dinner reservations.

It was a relief to sit down in another air conditioned restaurant. Although it was early evening, the heat was not backing down. It was aggravating how much energy the sun stole from my body just walking from one attraction to the next. It didn't matter how much water I poured in, my body kept absorbing it like I was a dried up sponge.

After collapsing in my chair, I thought back to the events of the day and realized that it hadn't been a *total lack of pleasure.* My family had actually shared a couple of family phobicless moments like the Buzz Lightyear ride and lunch in Cinderella's castle. And I was pretty confident now that if anyone was responsible for sabotaging our vacations, it was the member of our family with the least seniority.

I was secretively appreciative that my mother had made reservations for this eighteenth century restaurant where characters like Mickey, Minnie, Chip and Dale, and Goofy paraded around in their Colonial threads. But, I thought it was odd when the waitress brought our waters to the table without any menus.

Well, it turned out that there *were no menus* for dinner because it was family style. We would be served roast turkey with mashed potatoes and gravy with all the fixins, kind of like Thanksgiving where you pass the dishes around the table. When the waitress divulged the price of the meal, I noticed my mom tug on her ear lobe, and my step- dad rub the back of his neck like they both do when they are stressing, and I watched them give each other the, *we didn't want to spend this much money,* look. You know the look that every kid dreads seeing on their parents' faces, especially when you're on vacation. I could tell that my mom was angry at herself for not running an adequate background check on the menu and prices when she made the reservations. Luckily, my dad was too exhausted and hungry to quarrel, so we ate our delicious meal and took tons of pictures with the Disney characters (my favorite was with Goofy wearing his knickers and tri-cornered hat), and my parents pulled out their credit card. My family seemed pretty content by the time the last bowl was cleared from our table.

And that was when it occurred to me that we seemed to get along just fine when we were fed, watered, and in a comfortable environment. Even Megan seemed pretty harmless. What did I expect from a three-year-old Disney princess fan?

I felt like I'd spun and landed on the number eighty-seven in the game, Chutes and Ladders, plummeting me all the way down to the beginning of the game!

Chapter 15
On Your Mark, Get Set, GO!

If I'd had my way we would have ended our day right after dinner. My motto is,

"Quit while you're ahead". I don't like crowds, and it just makes sense to leave when there aren't a million people herding towards three exit gates. But my parents insisted that we stay for the Electric Parade *for Megan.* What choice did I have? They were the taxi cab back to my grandparents' home.

The parade didn't start until nine o'clock, but we could see through the restaurant windows that people were already lining the streets. My parents hurried us to an area near the park entrance where we could make a quick get-away, and wedged us in between several, salty, smelly kids on the overcrowded curb. My dad purchased a green glow necklace for Megan from one of the Disney paraphernalia carts, while Mother Nature waltzed up and down the street serving up large portions of humidity pie.

Megan was mesmerized by the shimmering spectacle of lights. Each float was decorated with thousands of

Christmas lights in different colors. Some floats were all red or blue or green, and carried her favorite characters: Cinderella, Belle, Arielle, Snow White, and of course, Mickey and Minnie Mouse. I think that my mom and dad had more fun watching Megan watch the parade than they did watching the parade themselves.

I began to sense my step-dad's anxiety, anticipating the mob that would be flocking towards the park's entrance as soon as the parade ended. My parents had devised a plan which included my dad clutching Megan, my mom carrying the fifty pounds of cameras, strollers, and souvenir purchases.... and Daniel and I frantically racing to keep up.

It was like someone raised a checkered flag as the final float rounded the corner. As soon as my dad spied the back tail lights, he directed us out of the park like a sergeant guiding his troops to safety. We quickly boarded the ferry, ahead of the pack.

While we waited for the ferry to fill, I stared across the way at the amazing palace sparkling against a dark, starless sky, and heaved a sigh of appreciation and relief. It seemed like only ten minutes had past since I saw the castle for the first time. Twelve surreal hours had come and gone. Had I really been there? I took one last look at the castle and snapped an awesome memory photo.

The pace was much different getting off the ferry. There was no rushing, no scurrying. The mood was the same as Christmas morning after presents have been opened. All the magic and anticipation was gone, fizzled out like a balloon whistling through the air, landing deflated on a chair. And instead of mounds of wrapping paper and bows scattered all over the floor, tons of Disney souvenirs peeked out of bulging backpacks and strollers. We boarded a trolley which delivered us to the section where our lonely vehicle had sat all day, anxiously awaiting our return.

Incredible relief flooded my body as I curled up in the back corner of the car and kicked off my shoes and socks to let my toes breathe. As I nestled my head against my squishy bed pillow, the day's events ran through my mind like one of those old projectors that shows one slide at a time, and you have to hit the advance button to move to the next frame. Even though I would have rather spent less time in Fantasyland and more time in Tomorrowland, at least now I knew the map of the park like an important hockey play for the next time we visited. And there would be a next time. I was sure of it, now that Megan knew that this place existed.

Now that I was familiar with the home ice and had discovered its strengths and weaknesses, I would return with a carefully concocted game plan and a teammate my own age...*next time.*

I looked forward to the rest of the week's events: golfing, swimming, and MGM Studios on Thursday.

Chapter 16
Bowling Anyone?

"We made bowling reservations for twelve o'clock," I overheard my mamaw's sing song voice announce from miles away. I was in the deepest sleep of my life when her southern drawl slowly pulled me out of my coma. Paralyzed from the neck down, and recovering from physical and emotional exhaustion, it took a few minutes before I rejoined my body wrapped in the fresh Downy sheets in my mamaw's queen size bed. The road trip and Mother Nature's excruciating heat had left my tank bone dry.

Sweet cinnamon rolls teased my senses as I struggled to understand the bowling reference. Without my consent, my brain began powering up and processing thoughts:

"Wait a minute. I thought Tuesday was our golfing and swimming day? Hmmm... Daniel." My mamaw was probably worried that Daniel might get too much sun too soon, and decided that bowling would be a fun, indoor, away from the piercing rays of the sun, activity.

My mind raced. I needed a plan. I could plead dehydration from the previous day's agonizing heat, and convince everyone to go ahead without me, *or* I could insist that since everybody else was already showered and dressed I would put them behind, and I didn't want to make them late. Oh, this was too much thinking before noon.

"Jerry… are you awake yet? We're going bowling in an hour," My mamaw was peeking through the door of the darkly shaded room.

I sat up rubbing my eyes, forcing my nocturnal body to adjust to daylight. "Sure, bowling sounds good to me." Was that *my* voice? Even though the room was comfortably air conditioned, I must have been experiencing another episode like the one at the Magic Kingdom. Everyone who knows me is VERY aware that I *always* wake up on the wrong side of the bed, requiring at least sixty minutes before interaction with another human or dog for that matter, but it was 11:00 *A.M.* and I was participating in the land of the living.

As I pulled my, *I need a vacation from my vacation,* teenage body out of the bed, a wicked smile cracked my concrete face as evil thoughts churned:

"Daniel, bowling? Uncoordinated, impatient, impossible to please Daniel… bowling?"

This unexpected event could prove more entertaining than the Haunted Mansion incident. I didn't need any further prodding. Within twenty minutes I was showered, dressed, and enjoying a warm cinnamon roll in my grandparents' kitchen.

Chapter 17
Twofer!

My mom treated us to two heaping scoops of dysfunction when she tag teamed with Daniel in making quite a fool of herself as well. She's not much for organized games. I think it has a lot to do with the fact that she's a teacher and she plays enough games during the school year with her students: games like, *Guess Why I Didn't Do My Homework,* and her favorite, *I Don't Have a Pencil So I Can't Do Any Work.* So when summer arrives, she really needs some, *me time* to recover from all the months she spends teaching fifth graders that the front side of the paper has the holes on the left hand side, and that, alot is actually *two* words (a lot).

I've been to some of her summer teacher parties where her friends pretty much just sit around eating lots of chocolate and Mexican dips, telling stories that are so funny my eyes water. They don't play cards; they don't play games; they can't. Their brains are mush. That's why there is summer vacation; to give teachers time to regenerate new brain cells.

So from the moment my mom tied the laces on her Lysol scented bowling shoes, she made it VERY clear that bowling was definitely not one of her, *me time*, choices. I knew my mom would have killed to be relaxing in a lounge chair near a pool, reading the latest Harry Potter book, but instead she was in a frigid, dark bowling alley wearing dorky, germ infested bowling shoes.

She was so discouraged that she couldn't even laugh at herself (she normally can't anyways), when she tripped over her feet, plunging the ball into the gutter. And what was even worse was that she couldn't even bring herself to *fake* enjoyment when my papaw asked if she was having fun. A painful scowl that screamed, "I HATE BOWLING!" had taken control of her face.

Megan, on the other hand, was ecstatic when my dad handed her the blue bowling shoes (her favorite color), and immediately chose a matching ball. She waltzed up to the black line and fired the ball down the alley like a professional softball pitcher. She was a natural! The bumper pads on her alley helped her rack up a high score, and she loved it! All of the senior citizens peered down at the Shirley Temple look alike commenting,

"Isn't she just the cutest little thing?"

But my mom and Megan were simply the previews before the, *Daniel Feature Presentation*. For the safety of all bowlers, Daniel had been forced to share the same bumper padded alley as Megan to prevent possible unprecedented bowling alley fatalities. Daniel wore his humiliation like a fire engine red t-shirt that read,

"Please let the earth open up and swallow me."

My Papaw jokingly reminded Daniel,

"Now make sure that you let go of that ball!"

I kept hoping that he would forget and go bouncing down the alley with his fingers still clutched inside the ball, but, being the brainiac that he is, he quickly caught on to the game, commanding his brain to send the message to his right hand that the ball needed to be released *before* it smashed into those embarrassing bumper pads.

Daniel moved in slow motion each time he wound up for his delivery, and there was a two minute lapse from his clumsy retrieval to his awkward release. Each time he plopped down on the bench, I shot him my arrogant, *I'm better than you,* look just quickly enough so that no one noticed but him. I was hoping to ignite his short fuse and spark a few inappropriate responses, but Daniel stayed strong and controlled, suffering through two hours of artificial enjoyment. His face wore the same inherited scowl that was plastered all over my mother's, and each time my Papaw asked if he was enjoying himself, I noticed his clenched jaw and back teeth grinding as he answered,

"Uh huh," with a forced higher pitch on the, *huh.*

It didn't help Daniel's pathetic situation when I bowled a 158 despite having only bowled twice in my life. I have that athletic ability that kids like Daniel hate, and it became painfully obvious that Megan had inherited it also, but the gene had skipped the middle child like a stone skipping across a pond.

I'm usually pretty good at every sport that I try; whereas Daniel excels at every *subject* he tries. We all have our talents, and fortunately for Daniel, his are all locked up in his brain. The kid will probably find a cure for cancer some day, or design a space ship to Jupiter making him a billionaire. I'll make sure that I'm on his good side by then.

As my family paraded through the dimly lit alley towards the red exit sign, several retirees grinned in the direction of the prancing princess accompanied by her doting mamaw and papaw, followed by the rest of her court playing follow the leader. All Megan needed was a crown, white gloves, and the Miss America wave to complete the picture.

While my eyes adjusted to the piercing rays of the outdoors, heavy, humid clouds surrounded me like the hyenas sizing up Simba as I gasped for fresh air. As I trudged across the steaming parking lot, I forced my eyes shut and imagined racing down the arctic hockey rink in Monroe, Michigan. Frosty air blew through me like a blizzard, and when I opened my eyes I realized it was just our car's air conditioning.

All of this back and forthing between overly-air -conditioned buildings and vehicles, and Mother Nature's wicked, wicked weather was turning my brain into a lump of spaghetti, a favorite before a game, but not when I needed every ounce of brain power to solve a mystery.

My game plan? A long afternoon nap in my mamaw's shaded guest room hugging those Downy sheets, followed by one of her delicious dinners. It wasn't much of a plan, but it was all my low batteried body could muster.

Chapter 18
Just Sit There and Eat It!

I love my step-dad's parents. They're just really nice people. I think that sometimes they feel badly because they don't live close enough to help my parents with babysitting and fixing toilets, and things like that. So when we visit they take us out to eat, and buy each of us little gifts like the golf shirt my mamaw bought for me which later became the world's most expensive paper towel.

I actually have the best of both worlds when it comes to grandparents. My Michigan grandparents come to my hockey games and Christmas programs, and make my favorite birthday cake: chocolate chip with raspberry filling, and my Florida grandparents give my family a nice vacation by welcoming us into their home for a week free of rent, utilities, and groceries, despite our disturbing displays of dysfunction. And this leads me to the grand finale of any family vacation we've ever had, or ever *will* have. I will remember this day forever. It was the day of the, *dreaded Daniel dinner.*

Wednesday had the *makings* of a pretty normal day. Golfing with my step-dad and papaw after an early lunch, (which just so happened to be my favorite mamaw recipe: baked ham and cheese pockets with Catalina salad dressing, topped off with barbecue chips and an icy cold Mountain Dew), and hanging by the pool seemed like a recipe for at least one day free of any vacation malfunctions.

After out-golfing both my step-dad and papaw in, shirt dripping, arm pits smelling like my hockey pants, heat we headed back to the house to meet up with Megan and Daniel who had been shopping with my mamaw. They were sitting at the kitchen table with their swimsuits on, poking and prodding one another, obviously impatient to begin the next event on the day's itinerary.

My mamaw eagerly presented me with a new polo shirt (she said the color was cream, but it looked white to me), so I hugged and thanked her, and was about to plunk my stinky, lifeless body on her floral couch when I noticed the intensity of my sibling's blows increasing. So, instead, I dragged my body into the bedroom, peeled of my clothes, and pulled on my swimsuit hoping to hurry my family out of the house and diffuse the two ticking time bombs.

My step-dad boarded my grandparents' golf cart and plopped Megan on his lap. Daniel squeezed in next to them and I jumped in the front seat next to my papaw. My papaw drove the golf cart like a NASCAR driver down to the family pool in their retirement community, while my mom rode over with my mamaw in their Dodge van.

Once there, my step-dad and papaw took turns dunking Daniel. It wasn't hard to lose sight of his glistening white torso. Every once in a while I would glide in just long enough to cool down, and then I would stretch out on a lounge chair to toast my tanned body. There wasn't too much in the babe department for a teenage boy to enjoy. Most of the babes were over sixty, wearing swimsuits that, in my opinion, didn't cover enough of their antique bodies.

Our Little Mermaid's tanned, tiny arms poked through yellow floaties in case she slipped out of my mom's or dad's arms. We kept taking turns holding her under a miniature Niagara Falls that dumped gallons of water on us. She loved the falls almost as much as she enjoyed showing off her wrinkled fingers and toes to my papaw who faked serious interest. If she'd had her way she would have splashed in the pool until sundown, so my papaw coaxed her out of the pool with the promise that she could sit in the front seat of the golf cart with him on the way home.

My step-dad had left earlier with mamaw when Mother Nature dealt him a dehydrating TKO. After battling an overheated golf course all morning, he'd decided the best place to recuperate was in a quiet, air conditioned house with a large supply of Coke and ESPN.

I tried to persuade my papaw to let me have a crack at driving the golf cart home, but his, "I don't think so, Jerry" seemed non-negotiable. I figured debating with a retired high school football coach, slash teacher, was a pretty hopeless situation.

After a parade of showers my family sprawled out all over the living room couches and carpeting. Megan was watching her Cinderella video for the fiftieth time, and the rest of us were pretty much in a comatose state. I was just starting to nod off when I was jolted by questions rocketing out of the kitchen,

Who wants salad? Do you like bacon on your salad? Eggs? Cheese? Tomatoes?" followed by,

"Dan, ask the kids what they want to drink," followed by, "Who wants milk? Coke? Diet Coke? Mountain Dew? Water? Iced Tea? With or without ice?"

Having to make so many decisions was exhausting. I would have been just as happy with a large bowl of Fruit Loops or a frozen pizza.

Weeks before our arrival, my mamaw had carefully planned each meal for our vacation, from the homemade chocolate chip cookies on her kitchen counter, to the delicious make ahead recipes from her library of church cookbooks. However, despite these organized menus, nothing had prepared her for this evening's surprise main course.

At this point I want to make it very clear that I appreciate all of the effort, care, and love that my mamaw has mixed into every chicken casserole, pot roast, and macaroni and cheese to come out of her apple themed, abounding in oak, kitchen. If my mamaw is reading this,

"I love you, Mamaw, and I am genuinely grateful for every morsel of food that you have ever prepared for my family; even if there is *one* among us who finds fault with your culinary skills."

"Just sit there and eat it!" my mamaw cackled.

The kitchen was so quiet I could hear the geckos breathing outside the front screen door. All eyes stared disbelievingly as every muscle in her tanned, slender face tensed while my, soon-to-be-dead, brother tactlessly questioned the identity of the gray and white particles swimming in the wide egg noodles. The evening's menu consisted of beef stroganoff, rolls, salad, and a dessert that Daniel had supervised and given his full approval of consisting of chocolate cake, whipped cream, and Heath candy bars.

Since our arrival, for whatever warped reason, Daniel had taken on the role of meal cop, policing every lunch and dinner menu, putting my Mamaw through a daily meal interrogation. Every morning, shortly after breakfast, Daniel could be overheard questioning,

"Will there be any mushrooms in the casserole tonight? What about onions? There won't be any of that white stuff (cream cheese or sour cream), mixed in, will there? You know I don't like those green things either, (green peppers and celery). I only eat corn, no green beans. I don't like salad. Are we going to have rolls or biscuits? I don't like beef. It's too stringy in my teeth," and on and on.

He'd even found fault with my favorite ham and cheese biscuit sandwich, so my Mamaw had made *his* without the special Catalina dressing inside. Day after day, my Mamaw had demonstrated the utmost control as she patiently addressed his rude and disrespectful inquiries. But after days of constant cross examination, she was driven to the breaking point, like a murderer caving from incessant badgering admitting,

"Yes, I did it! The dead body is buried under the pile of round steak, noodles, sour cream, mushrooms, and yes, onions!"

I couldn't believe my ears. My mamaw was losing it, and it was all Daniel's fault! Not only was this unexpected turn of events about to blow the top off of the bowling fiasco, but there was a strong possibility that this humiliating display might completely erase my ungrateful teenager episode from my parents' memories. I had never seen my mamaw so shaken in my life. My parents were visibly embarrassed and unsure of how to react. Neither spoke. In fact, no one spoke.

I didn't expect this sort of behavior from my brother; not because he is the most polite and sensitive kid ever to inhabit the planet, but because he's a genius. He really is. His rare book dependency requires Saturday visits to the library (following piano lessons), and birthday and Christmas requests for Borders gift cards. The freaky thing about Daniel's book dependency is that the titles that tower from the carpet to his mattress are not the typical five- hundred page books that you'd expect to see. Of course he's read the, *Harry Potter* books and those *Narnia* books, but he's also got books about, *Dumb Bunnies* and *Captain Underpants*, as well. So you'd think that somewhere in that pile he would have come across a book on, *Meal Manners for Dummies*!

How could he pull such high marks in behavior from September to June, and then dip so low in the summer months that an emergency parent conference would be necessary? At least *my* behavior was consistent throughout the twelve months: *Enjoys socializing and entertaining others.*

I stared opened mouthed, wondering what his reaction would be to my mamaw's uncharacteristic eruption. I could see the wheels turning in that oversize brain of his. Daniel is typically a good test taker, even pop tests, so I wasn't surprised when he started shoveling the beef stroganoff into his mouth like it was a bacon double cheeseburger.

I cringed watching him choke down the very mushrooms, onions, and other sworn enemies of his overly choosy taste buds. Well, I didn't need an invitation. I followed suit, and even asked for seconds, hoping to model the, *kiss up* behavior which my brother was so obviously lacking experience …and I made a mental note to avoid all of this embarrassing nonsense with my own offspring some day. I would just raise perfect children.

Chapter 19
Disturbing Thoughts

Not only had Daniel been downgraded to a category three on the, *Favorite Children List;* he'd also risen to the top of my, *Family Member Solely Responsible for Sabotaging Vacations,* list He'd been my original suspect from our first family theme park escapade five years ago, and I should have never cleared him. It's like when you bubble in 'C' on a test, and then go back and change it to 'A', and then when you get the test back you find out the correct answer was 'C'... I should have stuck with my first instinct.

What bothered me most about Daniel's disgraceful behavior was how he'd turned my sweet, mild mannered mamaw into Meal Mamawzilla. I never asked him about the, *behind closed doors session,* with our parents after his dreadful display of disrespect. But his behavior made me wonder, "If someone that smart could demonstrate such diabolical behavior, what devious displays was a guy like me capable of?" Unlike Daniel, I didn't get straight A's in school. My report card is proof that variety is the spice of life. I didn't like to admit, especially to myself, that I could probably get better grades if I spent more time with the books and less time with the pucks. And then there were the female distractions. There are slim pickins for a guy like me when most girls nowadays turn into Amazons before their thirteenth birthdays.

Thursday's trip to MGM Studios would give me the chance to really check out Daniel's behavior. Without Megan, my investigative camera would be better able to zoom in, not only on Daniel, but also my parents' role in this mystery as well. There were only two days left on a running clock, and I knew better than most, that anything can happen in those last few seconds of play!

Chapter 20
Vacation Variables

The local weather man informed us that our day spent at the Magic Kingdom with the three-year-old tyrant had registered one- hundred-five degrees on the heat index. Naturally, the Thursday morning of our next planned theme park visit proved to be a repeat performance of the same sinuous weather.

As I stuffed my reluctant legs back into our car, it was like I'd never left my assigned seat. Little stop signs halted blood flow to my feet before we turned out of my grandparents' retirement village. I placed my designated driving pillow against the window (this always makes my mom nervous, as if I'm going to fall out of a locked car door!), and resumed the restless sleep mode again to pass the sixty minute drive to MGM Studios.

I dreamed I was sitting in a white, sterile classroom, empty except for my sixth grade science teacher and me. She was lecturing the ghost class on variables, and I was actually paying attention as if she was setting up the play that would win our hockey team the state championship.

I began to think of our family as a unique science experiment with four variables:

The three-year-old variable had been left behind with my mamaw and mapaw for the day where she would be immersed in a variety of, *spoil me rotten* activities. These would include an initial showing off period to all of their friends who would think she was as precious as the blue diamond from the movie, *Titanic,* followed by a trip to her favorite fast food restaurant for chicken nuggets, fries, and a chocolate shake. Next, they would take her to feed the buffalo, purchase a new dress, purse, or pair of sunglasses, and end the day with a visit to a local ice cream parlor for a soft serve vanilla cone.

Variables two, three, and four were traveling with me. I hadn't given too much thought to my parents, especially after the deadly Daniel dinner, but the poor vehicle choice as well as their sporadic fire cracker episodes definitely presented a case against them. And I couldn't rule out my mother's obnoxious bowling display. Each had made some miserable contribution to the week's events, ruining what should have been magical moments with their dark storm clouds.

And every experiment needs a constant, which in this case, was me. Obviously, I was the most stable member of our struggling family. Science was beginning to make sense for the first time, and it was my destiny to find the fatal force that had interfered with our family outings for so long.

"We're here. Let's get this show on the road." My mother's announcement yanked me back into reality. Had I been dreaming about my science teacher and variables?

My smoldering feet battled the heat and humidity as they carried me across the blistering pavement towards the park's entrance. A tiny voice whispered, "Stay constant, stable, normal," and my dream revealed itself as if on a monstrous IMAX screen:

TEENAGE BOY UNCOVERS CAUSE OF FAMILY VACATION MALFUNCTION!

Still, I wondered, "Could there be *another* factor staring me down like a brutal face off, and if so, would I discover it in time to salvage the remainder of my family's vacation?

Chapter 21
Will the Normal Members of My Family Please Stand Up?

Any pleasurable memories of MGM Studios on that horrendously hot Thursday are masked like creamy, buttery potatoes trapped under thick, dark, bitter gravy, which leaves such a bad taste in your mouth that no amount of rinsing will allow you to enjoy the delicious contents buried below.

Picture the movie, *Dr. Jekyll and Mr. Hyde* and you've captured the massive mood swings that each of us experienced throughout our Meganless day. The heat aroused monster-like tendencies transforming us into rabid, foaming at the mouth dogs. Keep in mind that my family was always borderline Mr. Hyde, but the tormenting temperatures teased our tepid tempers like someone playing with the knobs on a gas stove, cranking the gas between the high and low settings. Four pans of impatience spilled over not long after our arrival. If it had been just a *few* degrees cooler and a *few* ounces less humid, the day may have turned out differently, but Mother Nature was in complete control of *this* game!

We strolled through the gates around 10:00 and headed directly to the infamous, *Twilight Zone Tower of Terror.* At first, we wondered if the ride was open since the roped off lines were deserted. We apprehensively followed the maze leading into the hotel, and soon discovered that there was only one family ahead of us, and that we would be joining them for this attraction's first ride of the day!

Awaiting the elevator's dreaded descent and the process of plummeting me through thirteen floors of total terror panicked me as much as, *being plummeted through thirteen floors of total terror.* I did my best to anticipate this monster's first move, praying that the big black bar that prevented us from being ejected and hurled to a gruesome death wouldn't be the one in a billion with the defective bolt. The abrupt descent, not a thirteen floor plunge, maybe four or five, scattered my thoughts and challenged control of those bodily functions that leave humiliating traces of fear on the seat.

We were suspended for an eternity before the dreaded dive that revealed the origin of the ride's name. It was the kind of drop that a restroom procrastinator quickly regrets. After a series of ascents and descents I felt the need to inventory various body parts. My head was disconnected, suspended on the thirteenth floor, awaiting the return of the rest of my body. When the ride was over I was secretly relieved. Although I agreed with the others that it was a very cool ride, I was thinking,

"I definitely do not want to go on that ride again." Once was enough for me. A second helping and I would need those electric heart shocker paddles that you see on shows like ER to jumpstart my ticker in between floors. I shot my mom the,

"Let's move on… *now*," look. It was only ten a.m. and there was an entire park to check out. Plus, I needed some serious recuperation time.

And that's when our family became as divided as the North and South (my step-dad is a Civil War buff and sometimes I accidentally pick up information). He and Daniel were rounding the ropes for another taste of terror while my mom and I remained planted on the steaming concrete. She waved them on, telling them to go ahead and that we would wait for them on a nearby bench, but they responded condescendingly that they would do whatever *we* wanted. The scene reminded me of my favorite Looney Toon cartoons with the Roadrunner and the Coyote. It was like my family was the pathetic Coyote and the conniving Roadrunner had just lit the fuse for a series of explosive dysfunctional episodes.

For a while we wandered aimlessly, following a mother who was studying show times from her trusty park brochure. My heart sank into my sweaty socks. I was hoping that our day would be a little more spontaneous without Megan. I was wrong. My mom was diligently devising a plan that would include the *Indiana Jones Stunt Spectacular, Great Movie Ride, MGM Studios Backlot Tour, Who Wants to Be a Millionaire* and for the grand finale, the six o'clock performance of, *Beauty and the Beast.* I couldn't see myself bragging to my friends the first day back to school, "Yeah, and my favorite part of our vacation was the live performance of Beauty and the Beast!" I'm sure that the guys would be begging me for every enchanted detail.

My mother's annoying agenda was hanging over my head like another gray storm cloud. There were enough schedules during the school year with hockey practices and games, and the last thing I wanted on my summer vacation was another schedule.

My mom had made 12:30 reservations for lunch at the Sci Fi Diner. Unfortunately, we needed to make sure that we arrived on time for this lunch date, and this stressed my parents out more than it should have. I just wanted to *do something;* but each time we found a show or a ride, it seemed that there was a conflict with our lunch reservation; and so we walked around the park, sort of wasting time, getting hotter and sweatier by the minute. It was like we needed cables to jump start our funometer. I was beginning to think that the culprits in the great, *lack of family fun whodunit,* were much older than three or eight.

My mom insisted that we get our pictures taken with Aladdin and Jasmine, (I nestled against Jasmine's long, black, silky hair while Daniel posed next to the dude dressed as Aladdin). Then we watched some middle aged couple nagging and yelling at one another in a street show. At first I didn't know they were part of an act, but when people around me started laughing, I realized that they were actors. I should have guessed from the actress's fiery red hair and high pitched annoying voice, and their 1950's clothes that they weren't your typical Disney park goers. Finally, the clock struck 12:15: check-in time for our reservation.

If lunch at Cinderella's castle was a goal, lunch at the Sci Fi Diner was a hat trick! The restaurant was a MASSIVE drive-in theater. Dorky black and white science fiction movies where any fool can figure out that the creature from the depths of the ocean is really a man wearing a rubber fish head, were showing on a humongous movie screen, and cars like the ones in the movie, *Grease, were actually booths* with juke boxes in each one! This was theeeeeeee coolest restaurant I had ever been to in my whole life! Just days before, I'd enjoyed dining in Cindy's humble palace, but this was a restaurant made for a teen with a need for extreme.

The car was our time machine, transporting us back five decades to an era I felt strangely connected. As soon as my boney bottom slid across the seat of that 1955, baby blue, Ford Fairlane, I knew I was making one of those memories I would remember some day when my hair is gray and I set my teeth in a glass jar beside the sink. I might not recall my name, but I would remember the feel of this Ford.

I couldn't peel my eyes away from the screen showing the movie, The *Blob,* as the waiter took our orders. I ordered a classic 1950's cheeseburger, fries, and the best chocolate shake in the world! My family phobic worries completely vanished as I sat slurping my ultimate shake, waiting for the next movie, *Attack of the Fifty Foot Woman.* I'd died and gone to burger heaven! I wanted to stay in this place forever sipping shakes, chowing down burgers, and enjoying, *You Ain't Nothin' But A Houndog,* blasting on my personal jukebox.

I knew that nothing could ever top this experience... and maybe that is why our afternoon took such a tragic nose dive, resulting in a tornado of game misconducts and the most severe display of dysfunction ever to contaminate Walt's magical kingdom!

Chapter 22
Meal Meltdown

Cinderella and Sleeping Beauty's fairy godmothers, as well as Aladdin's magical genie must have combined forces to help keep our engines running on fun fuel. As we exited the Sci Fi Diner, I felt a force guiding our family towards the lines for the Indiana Jones Stunt Spectacular. The next show was in fifteen minutes. We couldn't have planned this any better! It was almost the same feeling I'd had when we were able to stay on the Buzz Lightyear ride for the second go around. Unbelievable!

It was like the show *knew* she was competing against the Sci Fi Diner for the ultimate attraction as she attempted to ooh and ahhhh her spectators. The life-defying stunts were impressive, but I began tensing midway through the show when I noticed my mother casually pull the park's brochure out of her purse. At first she just held it in her lap, steady, keeping her eyes glued to the show. After several minutes, her eyes shifted downward without moving a muscle in her face. It was a pretty sly move. A few more minutes passed, and she shamelessly began studying the pamphlet, ignoring the show completely. She'd caved! She *had* to have an organized plan for the rest of the day!

As we merged into the crowded aisle she sputtered that we needed to high tail it over to the, *Backlot Tour* in order to wedge it in before, *Who Wants to Be a Millionaire.* I was back on that spiraling out of control carousel. Once again, the day was slipping away from me. It had been a breath of fresh air carelessly jumping in the Indiana Jones line, and fresh air was in short supply today as Mother Nature was treating us to an encore of record setting temperatures. I'd had a brief encounter with spontaneity, and I'd liked it. It was fun and exciting. Unfortunately, Mr. Hyde had taken control of my mother as she faked interest in the Harrison Ford look alike. Her anxious energy contaminated my exhilaration. I should have never left that baby blue, 1955, Ford Fairlane.

After a brief embarrassing episode at, *Who Wants to be a Millionaire,* where my mother took a picture of the game show host after being warned that photography was not allowed, and an attendant requested she put the camera away, there was a little time before we needed to stand in another line for the 6:00 performance of *Beauty and the Beast.* My mom suggested that we look for somewhere to eat and then added, *under her breath,*

"And Mamaw says that we should get to the amphitheater an hour early for the laser show."

The what? I didn't see that on the schedule. We were already wasting thirty minutes of our day in a line for a show I would only admit seeing if my lucky hockey stick was being held for ransom, and now she was scheduling another hour of waiting so that we could watch some lights in the sky? I suffered through twenty-one hours crammed in the back seat of a midsize car with two, stress me out to the max siblings, to spend my vacation waiting in hot crowded lines and parked on benches?

Little bombs went off in my over- heated head each time she spoke… "Let's eat now, even though I'm not hungry…*BOOM!* I know that you'd rather spend your time on more thrilling attractions, but we need to fit in Beauty and the Beast…. *BOOM!* People are already getting in line for the laser show. We need to hurry! ….*BOOM, BOOM, BOOM!"*

I was too hot to eat, too tired to stand in one more line, and too angry to park myself on a bench to watch adults dressed as teapot and candelabras!

A series of embarrassing events took place at this time that resulted in one of the worst cases of family dysfunction ever recorded. At Disney they would say it was, *of epic proportions.* Not even the Greek hero, Hercules, could have saved our family from ourselves.

An hour before the Belle and Gaston show my mother, quite unexpectedly, relinquished her unappreciated role as entertainment and dining director, turning the late afternoon dining dilemma over to… *my step-dad.* Taking herself out of the game at this point was evil and selfish, and a few other words that I will not share. I felt like suggesting she dine with her friend, Cruella, while my step-dad, Daniel, and I ditched her musical production.

This late afternoon substitution threw our whole family off balance. Although my step dad was accustomed to literally sitting in the driver's seat, this unanticipated shift in roles took him totally off guard. My mother had arranged all of our pleasurable dining experiences from

Cinderella's castle to the Liberty Tree Tavern, and most recently, the Sci Fi Diner. How could he compete with dinners that had taken weeks to plan?

We followed my befuddled dad through a crowded Sunset Boulevard jammed with every meal choice imaginable. Burgers, pizza, hotdogs, and ice cream stands lined the street, but my step-dad just kept walking. He didn't know what to do, and my mother was in her, *whatever* mode. So...we walked up and down, up and down the same path for like twenty minutes. At one point he was way ahead of us, rambling utterances that should not have been allowed in Walt Disney's 'G' rated theme park. If someone had been watching us they would have hauled all four of us off in a paddy wagon wearing jackets where the arms tie in the back. The headlines would have read:

FAMILY GOES INSANE OVER DINING DECISION!

I could read my step-dad like a book (although reading was an uncharacteristic activity for me). He didn't want to do the *Beauty and the Beast* thing, he needed an air conditioning break, he wanted to ride Tower of Terror another bazillion times, and the back of his neck was well-done. But, instead of suggesting a plan where he and Daniel could revisit the place that had begun our roller coaster of a day, he pouted and threw what I would call, an adult temper tantrum. It was not a pretty scene.

It's a shame that my brother and I had to witness such unfamily vacation behavior. I wasn't even hungry, although I desperately needed a super sized Mountain Dew!

After standing in another hot line, and choking down equally hot pizza around a steaming outdoor patio table, we trudged over to the nearby musical production which I found… unexpectedly easier to swallow than my pizza.

Miraculously, the entertaining music and slight summer breeze tamed each of our beast-like tendencies, sending each of us into trance-like states…but not for long.

Chapter 23
One Hundred Million Volts of Electricity and
Metal Bleachers?

Ominous storm clouds made their appearance as Belle and Gaston were taking their final bows. I assumed that my mother would cancel the last event on her itinerary due to inclement weather. After all, teachers are more used to cancellations than any other profession. I was sure that she would treat this thunderstorm as seriously as a fog delay or snow day, and so I was shocked when she continued to guide us towards the amphitheater for the 9:00 showcasing of *Fantasmic*.

Oversized raindrops pelted the pavement like hundreds of water balloons as Mother Nature called out her most menacing cumuli nimbus clouds (I do pay attention in Science class), to bully us into retreat. The sudden change in weather seemed to have little effect on the Disney diehards waiting in line for the laser show. They continued to crowd into the exposed amphitheater, and so we joined them, despite all warnings that might conflict with common sense. The phrase, "If all your friends jumped off a bridge, would you?" came to mind.

My mother led our reluctant troop into an open row of metal bleachers in the midst of the fast approaching electrical storm. **METAL BLEACHERS AND ELECTRICLA STORM.** Hundreds of foolish fanatics had plunked on the well known conductors of electricity, showing no concern whatsoever for the fatal combination of metal and lightning. Even I was familiar with Ben Franklin's discovery of electricity and lightning from my fifth grade Social Studies.

"*Hello?!*" I felt like shouting, "Mr. Lightning is going to have a field day when he spots all of these ignorant spectators camped out on one of his favorite campgrounds!"

I looked around for a camera. Maybe we were all being videotaped on one of those, *America's Funniest Home Videos,* only this segment was entitled, *America's Stupidest People.* Was everyone under the false impression that they had been granted electrical shock immunity, because it was more like a group rate on electric chairs from where I was sitting. I wondered if Mr. Disney had some kind of agreement with Mother Nature that she overlook his little piece of heaven when it came to lightning strikes. I knew that Mamaw really wanted us to experience this spectacular show, but at the expense of leaving in body bags? We were sitting ducks on a pond of one hundred millions volts of electricity.

This was the end. We were all going to die here. This experiment would end the same way my science fair plants did when I fed them too much caffeine. One day they were thriving and at the top of their game, and the next day they were at the bottom of the classroom waste basket, the result of a Mountain Dew overdose.

Should I voice my concerns? I remembered what happened the last time I kept information to myself. What would it matter anyway if I fell to last place on the popularity list with my parents? I'd rather be last, than dead last. And why was *I* the only person in my family entertaining these morbid thoughts? It would have been more natural for one of the two college grads or the brain child to suggest the deadly repercussions of combining a well known electrical conductor with mega bolts of lightning.

"I can't believe we're sitting here waiting for lightning to strike us on these metal bleachers!" I spilled. "Don't you people know that metal is a conductor of electricity? This is the stupidest thing we've ever done!" I spurted like champagne on New Year's Eve.

There was no doubt that Daniel agreed our situation was a death sentence because he gave me the same appreciative look he'd shot me at the Haunted Mansion after saving his life earlier in the week. We shared a moment before the sky opened up like a waterfall, plunging gallons of water. We looked like we'd just stepped out of a shower with our clothes on when my step dad announced, "That's it. We're out of here," and it was clear that this was nonnegotiable. We bolted for the parking lot, but to my surprise, not many others followed. Did they all know something that we didn't? I didn't care. I wasn't willing to ride this storm out. With our luck, there was probably a tornado lurking in the alcove for act two.

Relief spread from my head to my toes as I rested my head against the back seat. My step-dad maneuvered our vehicle out of the parking lot, fighting zero visibility, while our Taurus's windshield wipers struggled to mop the rain out of her eyes. I knew he was thinking what a wash out this vacation had been, driving through two days of tormenting weather, and now, once again, battling the forces of nature.

Mother Nature made herself quite comfortable on the roof of our Taurus with her friend, Niagara Falls, under an immense, pink and white polka dotted golf umbrella, sipping raspberry iced tea, while mega- stress saturated the inside of our car as my drained dad battled for control of the steering wheel.

Well, it turned out the Disney fans did know something that we didn't. Florida is known for its afternoon showers, followed by skies as crystal blue as cats' eyes on a fat, white, fluffy, cat. The joke was on us. If we'd taken cover in one of the shops at Disney for about twenty minutes or so, we could have enjoyed the once in a lifetime laser show. Instead we had bolted.

What a surprise. Hidden behind door number one was the red Ford Mustang Convertible. My parents chose door number two... a year supply of broccoli.

Chapter 24
Case Closed?

We left early on a Saturday morning, seven days after our earth shattering arrival. My Mamaw cried, (although I wasn't sure if they were tears of sadness or relief), and my Papaw said,

"Now drive safely and have a good trip home," and that was it. Our vacation was officially over. A layover in a hotel tonight, and we'd be back on the road again tomorrow for the remainder of our drive back to Monroe.

Hours later, I jerked out of a restless sleep like a hard body slam where you come up seeing stars. Excruciating heat… torrential downpours… suffocating humidity… I sat up and stared unblinkingly out the window, forcing my brain to retrieve ten years of family vacations.

I pulled up files of trips to the zoo, water parks, and church festivals. Every maddening, miserable, mishap that our family ever experienced during this vacation and past excursions had been the evil doings of a culprit so subtle, that only the cleverest of teenagers could link the significant role *she* had played in unraveling the loose thread which eventually left a hole the size of the Grand Canyon in our fun family getaways. How could I have been so clueless?

From the Kentucky highway hammering, to the MGM studios near death experience, *Mother Nature,* had always been there aggravating our lives with her annoying heat and humidity, or endangering us with her lethal lightning and deadly downpours. Although each of my family members had had their suspicious moments, my family's shenanigans may not have been as defeating if *she* hadn't escalated each episode with her aggravating elements.

Sprinkling her destructive dust over our unsuspecting family was probably a time filler in between swallowing up houses in one gulp, spinning cars like toy tops, and hurtling tons of snow down her majestic mountains. Taking on an opponent of this magnitude would have been like the Detroit Red Wings facing off against a peewee team.

I started thinking. How many other families had experienced similar vacation woes? We couldn't be the only family on this twirling turntable of a planet that she had crippled with her destructive forces. There were probably thousands of families, too ashamed and embarrassed to reveal their own shocking tales of family vacation misery.

Perhaps my story will help others to realize the naked truth: Family vacations are, well, just that, vacations *with your family,* and families aren't perfect; so how could a teenager expect a perfect vacation like the one in the Disney commercial? It's interesting how *that* family wasn't bickering and pouting or sweating buckets of perspiration from the suffocating heat. That father's shirt wasn't glued to him and the mother wasn't lugging around fifty pounds of baggage. Mother Nature's spellbinding effects hadn't taken control of *that* family's minds and bodies. And instead of gray, foreboding clouds, Cinderella's castle had been surrounded by a blanket of blue, cloudless skies.

My family wasn't family phobic and there was no family member responsible for our lack of family vacation bliss. Mother Nature had been the silent *saboteur,* a variable I had never considered until now. My mind was flooded with understanding and my investigation quickly concluded like a famous whodunit mystery.

Early the next morning, before I forced my legs (Hey, had I grown another inch?), into the backseat of a vehicle who had gone from rookie to pro racer in the longest week of her life, I tilted my head upwards towards the cloudless sky and grinned. A slight breeze blew through my sun streaked hair. It was a perfect day, seventy-five degrees and not an ounce of humidity.

Tonight, I'd be home in my own bed, with a two liter bottle of Mountain Dew at my side, enjoying some video games or e-mailing my friends about the *perfect parts* of our vacation (Hey, they didn't need to know everything!). But for now, I huddled against the door, resting my head against the brand new, lucky golf shirt that my Mamaw bought for me, smirking with satisfaction that I'd solved the mystery of our family vacation malfunctions.

And Megan and Daniel, unaware of my clandestine investigation, and too naïve to understand how imperfect this family vacation had been, were squished into their assigned seats, already sleeping away the hours before a pit stop at one of our favorite breakfast restaurants, the Cracker Barrel.

And Mother Nature? She whipped up the family special: a sunshine skillet free from all green and white chewy things, with a side order of hope and anticipation for our next family vacation.

Literature Opportunities for the Classroom

This story provides an excellent opportunity for setting up journal writing: more specifically, literature response journals, with your students at the beginning of the school year. Add one or two spiral notebooks to your classroom supplies list before school begins to ensure most students have notebooks the first day. Help students set up a, *Family Vacation Malfunction,* notebook and choose from the following activities for students to participate in throughout the story. Students may create separate sections for illustrations, predictions, character analysis, and their personal vacation narratives. When students share their vacation experiences, encourage them to share photographs with their classmates as well!

Figurative Language References - Students will illustrate one or two examples of figurative language from each chapter.

Hockey References - Students will record page numbers and examples of the many references to the game of hockey throughout the story.

Alliteration References: The author enjoys using alliteration throughout the story. Students may record the many examples of alliteration.

References to Mother Nature: Students may identify and/or illustrate the references made to various types of storms. This particular section will prove helpful at the end of the story.

Chapter Predictions: Using chapter titles, encourage predictions based on title clues.

Character Analysis: Using a Venn diagram, students may compare and contrast the two brothers in the story. Discuss how their relationship changes throughout the story.

Compare/Contrast: Students may compare/ contrast themselves with a sibling and share with the class.

Research/Biography: Megan is referred to as a, "Shirley Temple look alike". Students may research Shirley Temple. Show a Shirley Temple movie to the class!

Writing Activity: The author deliberately chose to move her story from the Thursday evening storm to the Saturday morning departure. Students will write Chapter 23 ½ in which they describe events which could have occurred on Friday.

Writing Activity: Upon completion of the story, students may write short narratives of their own family vacations malfunctions. Encourage students to read their narratives aloud to their classmates.

About the Author

Anita Passon lives in Monroe, Michigan with her husband, three children, and Yorkshire, Reese. She earned her Bachelors and Masters of Education degrees from the University of Toledo in Toledo, Ohio. She has taught elementary school for seventeen years, with fifteen years in fifth grade. She enjoys watching movies with her family, baking, and singing for her church. Ms. Passon looks forward to writing a sequel to, *Family Vacation Malfunction*, as told through the eyes of an older and wiser female sibling.

2679620

Made in the USA